The Magical Life of Mr. Renny

LEO TIMMERS

TRANSLATED BY BILL NAGELKERKE

GECKO PRESS

This edition first published in 2012 by Gecko Press
PO Box 9335, Marion Square, Wellington 6141, New Zealand
info@geckopress.com

Original title: Meneer René
Copyright text and illustrations © 2010 by Leo Timmers, Amsterdam, Em. Querido's Uitgeverij B.V.

First American edition published in 2012 by Gecko Press USA, an imprint of Gecko Press Ltd.

A catalog record for this book is available from the US Library of Congress.

Distributed in the United States and Canada by
Lerner Publishing Group, Inc.
241 First Avenue North
Minneapolis, MN 55401 USA
www.lernerbooks.com

Distributed in the UK by Bounce! Sales and Marketing

Translated by Bill Nagelkerke
Edited by Penelope Todd
Typeset by Tabitha Arthur
Printed by Everbest, China

A catalogue record for this book is available from the National Library of New Zealand.

The translation of this book was funded by the
Flemish Literature Fund (www.flemishliterature.be).

ISBN hardback: 978-1-877579-20-2
ISBN paperback: 978-1-877467-89-9

For more curiously good books, visit www.geckopress.com

This is not an apple.

It's a painting of an apple.

Mr. Renny was such a good painter that whatever he painted looked just like the real thing.

Every week he trundled his paintings to the market.

Rose's stall was always bustling.
She sold bananas, strawberries, and lemons by the dozen.

But no one wanted to buy Mr. Renny's paintings. Not even the one of the apple.
"If only I could eat it," he sighed. "Then I wouldn't be so hungry."

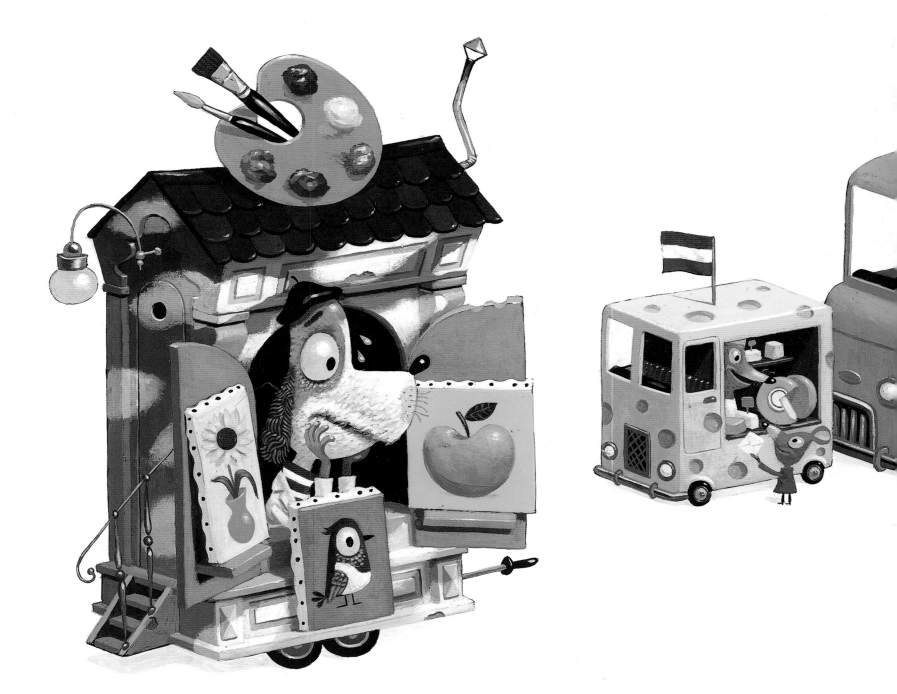

"You want to eat the apple?" a stranger asked. "You can, you know."
The man snapped his fingers and—POOF!—the apple was real.
"Take a bite and all your paintings will come to life," said the man.

"Wh-who are you?" asked Mr. Renny. But the man was already gone.
Mr. Renny hesitated a moment, then bit into the apple.
Unbelievable! All his paintings sprang to life.

Mr. Renny raced home
to start a new painting at once.

With the final brushstroke it turned into...

...a real hotdog.

Delicious!

And so was the dessert.

Mr. Renny had always wanted a car.

He drove to Rome, Paris, Brussels, and through the tunnel, all the way to London. But all the time he was imagining what he could do next.

He'd always dreamed of going to sea.

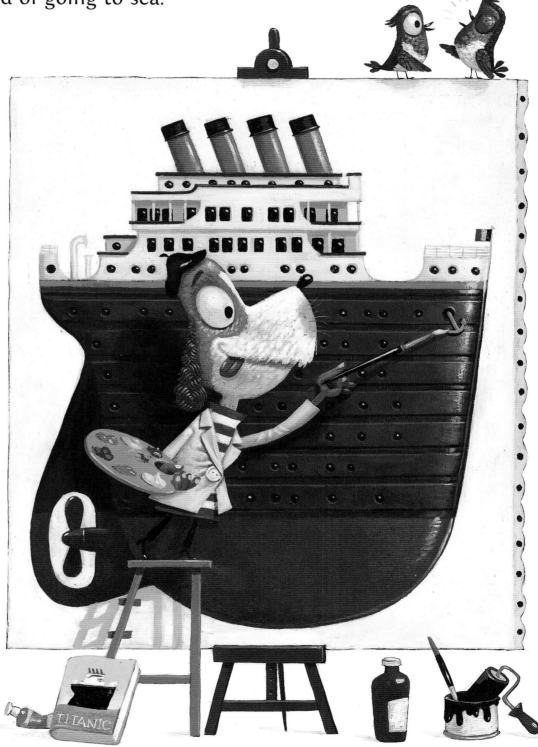

But he soon lost interest in life on the ocean. On board his ship, Mr. Renny could think only of his next painting.

There were still so many things he wanted.

a vase another car perfume champagne

a swimming pool a plane

more champagne a silk suit a radio

a bed a lamp a banquet a blimp

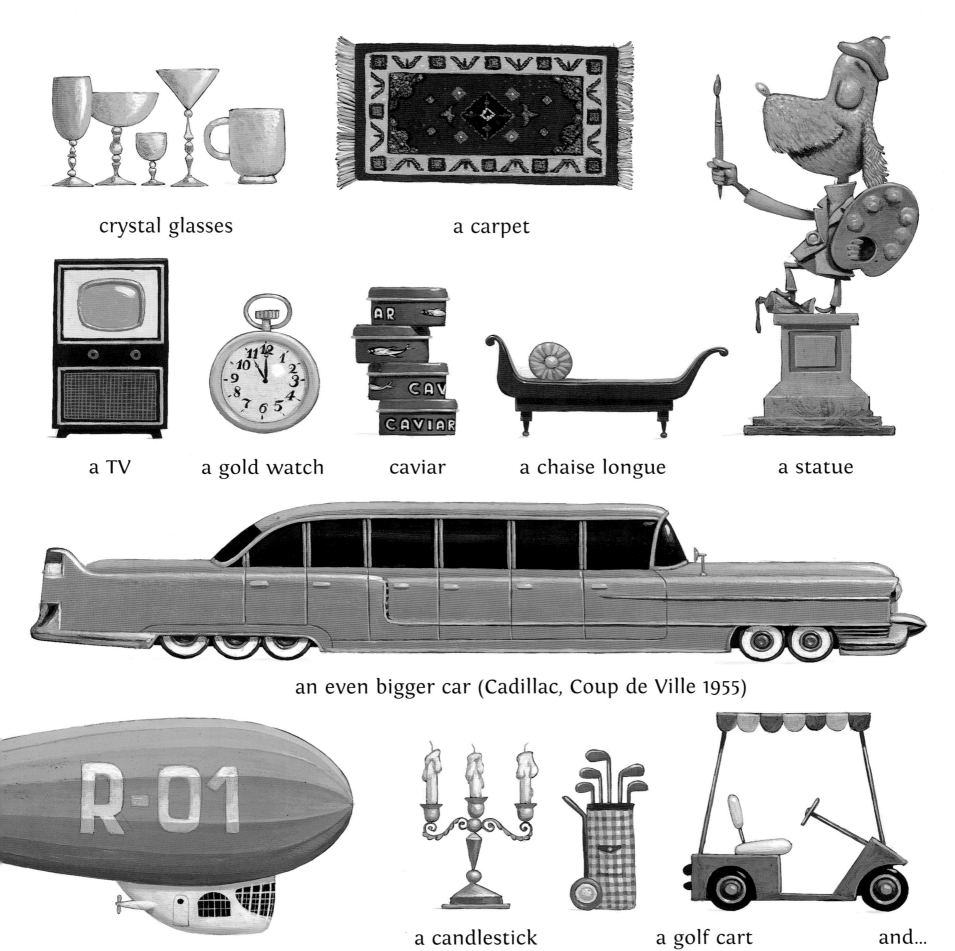

crystal glasses

a carpet

a TV

a gold watch

caviar

a chaise longue

a statue

an even bigger car (Cadillac, Coup de Ville 1955)

a candlestick

a golf cart

and...

...a mansion!

Just as Mr. Renny was wondering what he should paint next—his own amusement park, or a rocket to the moon, perhaps?—the doorbell rang.

It was Rose. "Hello," she said.
"I've come to buy one of your paintings."

"I'm sorry, Rose, but they're
all gone," said Mr. Renny.

"Can't you paint one just for me?"
"I'm sorry, Rose. I really can't."

"So you're no longer a painter?
What a pity, Mr. Renny.
In that case, I'll be on my way."

What now?

Mr. Renny thought long...

...and hard.

That's it!

"Will you help me one more time?" he asked the man.
"I want to paint an ordinary picture again.
One that doesn't come to life."

"I thought this would happen," laughed the man.
He snapped his fingers.

Just like that, everything vanished.
The cars, the swimming pool, the ship.
They all turned back into paintings.
Mr. Renny didn't mind a bit.
He already knew what he wanted to paint next.

He finished the painting and...nothing happened.
Overjoyed, Mr. Renny rushed to the market.

"You're back!" Rose smiled.
"I have a surprise for you." Mr. Renny held up his new painting.
 Rose was thrilled. "But I thought you weren't a painter any more?"

"Of course I am," said Mr. Renny.
"Once a painter, always a painter!"

For Rose